Earth
Alert

Invasion from the Time-Zone

Anthony Sailer

authorHOUSE®

AuthorHouse™
1663 Liberty Drive
Bloomington, IN 47403
www.authorhouse.com
Phone: 1-800-839-8640

Published by AuthorHouse 2/07/2014

ISBN: 978-1-4918-4218-8 (sc)
ISBN: 978-1-4918-4217-1 (e)

Library of Congress Control Number: 2013922380

Stage 1 ✦

Premonitions

"Hurry Steve! We have to seal off the transporter to keep anyone else from coming!"

"Todd, there's a group coming from across the field, they're headed right for us!"

"Alright Kevin, get Trevor back here so we can reassemble the group!"

"I can't get to him Todd, there's too many warriors in the way!"

"Trevor! Trevor get over here! We have to retreat! Get back to my apartment!"

"I can't Todd! I need help they're trying to surround me!"

"Dad!"

"What Chrissy!?"

"I need help!"

"Dad!"

"What Josh!"

"There's more coming from the building by the pool!"

"Damn it! Steve, you and Kevin try to get Trevor! I need to get Chrissy and Josh!"

"Todd I'm free! I'm headed for the wishing well now!"

"Good Trevor, I have Chrissy and Josh, let's go! Everyone back up to my apartment!"

"Todd they're trying to block the entrance to the building!"

"Damn it Steve!" Everyone head for the back entrance, hurry!"

"Todd watch out, there's three warriors coming out from behind the dumpster!"

"I see them Steve! Everyone hurry, get to that door! Let's go, let's go!"

"Dad, I've been hit!"

"Steve get everyone upstairs, Chrissy's been hit! I'll get her then meet you upstairs!"

"Alright Todd!"

"Chrissy here I got you, let's get upstairs."

"Alright, thanks dad."

"Steve! Steve! Get that transporter off-line!"

"I'm trying Todd, the panel isn't responding!"

"Have Trevor help!"

"Hey Todd its Trevor, everything's froze up, nothing is responding for me either!"

"Todd its Steve again, there's been a surge in the transporter! Tell him Trevor!"

"Steve's right Todd, this thing's going to blow!"

"Todd its Kevin, there's no way to stop it! We need to get the hell out of here!"

"Transporter malfunction. Destruct sequence in progress. Ten…nine…eight…seven…six-"

"Steve get everyone out now! Go! Go! Go! Hurry!"

"Three…two-"

"No!"

Beep! Beep! Beep! Beep! "Dad! Turn your alarm clock off," Christina hollered from her room. "Huh, what," I mumbled as I barely opened my eyes. I was completely disoriented then I finally heard my alarm clock blaring, so I jumped up and turned it off.

"Thank you," Chrissy hollered to me, still in her room.

"What were you screaming about?"

"What are you talking about Chrissy?"

"You were screaming no, no, no, and yelling to get out."

"Oh ok…um…I don't remember." That wasn't true though, I did remember, I just didn't want her to know. I thought if I told her that I had a nightmare related to our explorations that I would scare her away from any future journeys. "Thanks for waking me up dad," Josh yelled from the living room. "Sorry, you both go back to bed." "Gladly," Josh yelled back. "Definitely," Christina hollered from her room then everyone got quiet.

The kids didn't spend the night very often now that they were older. My apartment was only a two bedroom, so when they did Josh always slept on the Futon in the living room. Since they were going back to sleep I sat up on the edge of the bed to think about the nightmare I just had. It had been a long time sine I had dreamt about anything like that. It was almost like a newer version of an invasion like the one from long ago. In a way it felt like a premonition, but I couldn't figure it out. Unless warriors had found a way to leave the twelfth dimension, as well as their universe, there was no possible threat to our world. After sitting up a few minutes, I decided to lay down to go back to sleep.

Stage II

Nightmares

It was 9 a.m. Saturday when we woke up for the day. I went to the kitchen then poured a cup of coffee and lit up a cigarette as I walked into the living room. Josh sat up from the Futon saying he was hungry. I reminded him to check his sugar and take his insulin before he ate. As he got up to go into the dining room to test his sugar I turned on the computer. Typically I would play pinball for an hour or so as I would wake up listening to the television, but when the kids were over I let them take control of the television. A few minutes later Chrissy came out into the living room asking if she could play the Playstation. I said yes and then she picked out a game and started playing. Josh came over to show me his meter so I could see what his sugar level was then he went into the kitchen to grab his usual breakfast, which was Frosted Fudge Pop Tarts.

While Josh sat at the dining room table to eat, Chrissy continued playing the Playstation while I played pinball. About twenty minutes later my cell phone rang and I could tell by the ringtone that it was Steve, so I paused my game and picked up. He asked what was going on while telling me that he had just woke up a short time ago and was on the computer drinking his coffee. I told him what we were all doing then we chatted for awhile.

He asked if we had anything going today, because if not he wondered if we wanted to come up for the day. I told I wish I could but we had a bunch of stuff to do so we wouldn't be able to come up. Sounding disappointed he said ok, then said he had to get going. I told him maybe I'd give him a call later that night and said goodbye. Once I got off the phone I started getting hungry so I quit my game to go grab some cereal. Josh was done eating so I sat down to eat while Josh got on the computer to start playing a game.

After I finished eating Chrissy said she was hungry, so she went into the kitchen to make some eggs, as she usually did when she was over. Josh hopped from the computer to Playstation as I went back on the computer to play more pinball. The weekend mornings when the kids were over often went like this, playing musical chairs while we rotated to keep ourselves occupied with our limited entertainment. About forty-five minutes later I decided to take a shower so I got up to leave the living room as Chrissy took my place at the computer.

After I got ready for the day it was Chrissy's turn as Josh took her place. Once she was finished, Josh went to get ready as Chrissy took his spot. Around 12:30 p.m. we took off for the day since I had a bunch of errands to run. About 5:30 p.m. we were headed back to my place, but we stopped at a drive-thru to take some food home. Once we finished eating we agreed on a diversion and decided to watch a movie. About 9:45 p.m. when the movie was finished my cell phone rang, it was Kevin. I went over to my glider chair to talk to Kevin while the kids went back to playing games. Kevin and I talked for almost two hours before we got off the phone with each other. By this time Chrissy was getting tired so she went to bed. Josh wasn't tired, but as I often had to, I told him it was time for bed.

I got my coffee ready for the morning then went to my bedroom. I was tired but I wasn't quite ready to go to sleep, so I played Chrissy's keyboard for forty-five minutes or so. Finally about 12:35 a.m. I turned off the keyboard, turned off the light, and crawled into bed. I started dozing off while visualizing myself in the fourth dimension just walking around and looking at everything. Eventually the vision faded to darkness as I fell asleep. I then started dreaming, a similar dream to the one I had the previous night.

It was the same setting, all of us were in the field across from my apartment and we were running back to my bedroom to shut sown the transporter. Warriors from one of the dimensions were here on Earth trying to take over our world. They were everywhere, overpowering us while blocking us from entering the apartment building. We were then separated from each other and we couldn't regroup, then all of a sudden everything changed. We were all at the street entrance that led to my apartment complex. It was very foggy to where we couldn't see to the other end of the street. We were walking slowly down the street toward my apartment complex as we all had our energy rifles drawn, as if to defend ourselves.

There were two side streets off to the right that we would pass before we would reach the wishing well directly in front of my building. As we approached the first side street it looked as if something was glowing off in the distance. We kept walking as Steve, Kevin, and Josh watched the left side of the street since there several apartment buildings from another apartment complex before mine. It was very quiet as we continued walking with no sounds of cars, no birds, no wind, nothing. We got to the second street where the offices to the other complex were and there was also a pool where the street dead end. Looking down that street it looked like there were more things glowing inside the fence that surrounded the pool. We stopped for a moment as we took a closer look, but we didn't pursue and kept walking toward the wishing well.

We were almost to the wishing well when everything started to fade to a solid white, then I woke up. I sat up quickly and was breathing fast then I threw the covers off of me as I wiped the cold sweat off my face. I didn't make any noise so I wouldn't wake up the kids as I sat there in the darkness while I drank my bottled water and lit up a cigarette. Why was I having nightmares all of a sudden! There was no threat to Earth and we were in no danger! I couldn't understand it and just shook my head as I stared across my dark bedroom.

When I finished my cigarette and my water I laid back down and tried to fall back to sleep. I peeked at the clock before I shut my eyes; it was 3:30 a.m. I finished the night peacefully until I woke up at 7 a.m. The kids were sound asleep so I quietly walked into the kitchen where I poured a cup of coffee. Afterwards I went back into my room, took a couple sips of coffee, and sat on the edge of my bed just staring across the room. I stayed in there quite awhile trying to figure out why I was having these nightmares. I must have been in a deep trance since I didn't notice Chrissy pop her head in the doorway.

She hollered dad so loud I jumped as I turned around and fell off the edge of the bed. "Dad, I've been calling you for five minutes and you never answered," she said. "I'm sorry I didn't hear you. What did you want Chrissy?" "I just wanted to say good morning." "Oh…um, good morning." She entered my room then sat down on the edge of the bed at the far end. I got back up and sat down on the bed too, and we started talking. A little while later Josh came in the doorway barely awake and mumbled, "You guys woke me up." "Sorry," we both said then went back to talking. "I'm hungry dad." "Josh, go test and eat."

He turned around and lurched down the hallway toward dining room table where he kept his test kit. Chrissy and I got up to take our conversation to the living room. A little while later she and I grabbed some breakfast, then got ready for the day. We didn't have anything special planned so we were just going go kick back and hang out. I was supposed to take them home mid afternoon as opposed to the typical Sunday evening.

They had something going on with their mom, so she asked me to bring them home early. It wasn't a big deal to me as it would give me a chance to get some much needed laundry done. It was almost lunch time when I got a call from Trevor. He just called to see what I was up to. He also asked if I had any trips, as he called them, planned anytime soon. I could tell by the tone in his voice that he was itching to get back to the time-zone. I told him maybe the following weekend we could get away. He said ok then he let me go.

Chrissy and I made lunch for the three of us then we ate. We spent the next couple of hours playing games before I got ready to take them home. Once I dropped them off and got back home, I went ahead with doing my laundry. After I finished, I cleaned up the apartment a little.

Stage III ✦ ✦

A New Threat

I decided to do a systems check on the transporter when I noticed on the control panel that the signal from the fourth dimension was flashing, which indicated that Phenom was trying to contact me. This was the first time the signal had been used since Sempron and I developed it. I thought something might be wrong so I quickly powered up the transporter. I grabbed a few basic weapons along with a quick snack as I waited for the activation to complete. Once it was ready I stepped in, set coordinates then energized the transporter as I was off to see Phenom.

Once I arrived in the fourth dimension I quickly checked things out at our headquarters then made my way to see Phenom. A short time later when I reached the city I call upon Athlon to inform her that I was here to see Phenom in response to his signal. She said that it was urgent that he speak with me so she quickly led me to him. Once we got to him Athlon departed while Phenom invited me to sit down as he told me he had some information to pass along. I sat down while I closely paid attention to what he had to tell me. He informed that there was a new threat, a new adversary from the sixth dimension, and that their leader's name was Denon.

Phenom described them as an energy warriors species nearly identical to themselves here in the fourth dimension, only more powerful. I asked him how he knew all this when he answered by telling me that a short time ago Denon was here with a squadron of warriors. Phenom further explained that Denon was here to announce their return to power as they were destined to find those responsible for the destruction of the seventh dimension, along with the devastating effects it had on their world in the sixth dimension. Phenom also said that he believed they may be able to travel outside this time-zone.

I asked him what made him think that. He said he had no proof; it was just something he sensed. He hoped that he was wrong, but he just wanted to warn me about what had happened. I thanked him for the forewarning as I got up, then I asked Phenom to please inform me if anything else happened since I needed to return to Earth. We bid each other farewell, then I opted to transport back to Earth from the city. I arrived back on Earth just before dinner time. When dinner was finished I called Steve to let him know what I had just learned. Afterwards I called Kevin, then Trevor. I would tell the kids when it was necessary, but not before since I didn't want to inflict any unnecessary stress on them.

A couple of hours later I decided to go and finish checking the systems on the transporter in my room. By the time I finished checking the systems it was getting late so I decided to go to bed. Once I made up my coffee for the following morning I took my usual handful of items to my bedroom with me which consisted of cigarettes, lighter, bottled water, and cell phone since I did not have a land line. I turned on my alarm clock, turned off the lights then crawled into bed. As I pulled the covers up to my chin and closed my eyes, I hoped that tonight would be a peaceful nights rest. I tossed and turned for a little while before settling down as I began to drift off to sleep.

Stage IV ✦

The Past

Knock! Knock! Knock! I heard the front door pounding so I got out of bed. I glanced at the alarm clock behind me on my headboard to see that it was 7:30 p.m. It was just getting dark when I looked through the vertical blinds out of my bedroom window. I stepped out into the hallway, turned right, cut through the kitchen, and turned left into the foyer to go answer the door. I opened the door to see that it was Mark; then I opened the door wider where I saw everyone else. Mark, Dan, Jeff, Herb, Andrew, Jack, "Melvin," Trevor, Wayne, and Bob were all standing on my front porch waiting on me. "Dude, we've been knocking for ten minutes," Mark said. "Sorry, I kinda fell asleep on my waterbed." I opened the door to let them all in.

Once inside we headed down to my basement to hang out. The basement was completely finished and all five of my keyboards were down there. The basement is where I spent a lot of my time, not to mention all my cassette tapes, along with my boom box were down there too. We got downstairs then started talking. They were asking me if we were still going to the fourth dimension tonight and I answered yes that we were leaving at 10 p.m. Mark mentioned that we should start double checking our weapons. I agreed that we should start soon then we continued talking. "We need to destroy the core to stop Mutane once and for all," Jeff said. Everyone else yelled out in agreement as they were getting anxious.

I mentioned that we would not contact Toron unless it was absolutely necessary. Mark also mentioned that if anything happened to where we couldn't make it back to Earth, to head to the seventh dimension and take shelter there. Everyone understood and agreed then we headed back upstairs to my room. We had talked for awhile when I noticed it was 9 p.m. As soon as we got in my room the group started checking their weapons as I headed for my attached bathroom to check the transporter. Once I activated it I called Jack in there so he could make any necessary adjustments. As he began doing that I went back into my room where I began checking my weapons along with the others.

We finished about 9:30 pm then we went into the kitchen to grab something to eat before we left. Things had changed since earlier, I wasn't sure how, but they just felt different. Things then changed again as we weren't in my kitchen anymore, but instead we were in the field across from my house breaking off from a meeting. We were walking by the field when an energy blast came flying out of nowhere and nearly fried me. I looked to see there were warriors in various places firing at us so we scattered as I hid behind a nearby dumpster. They continued firing while during this time I told everyone to go get their alternate weapons from their houses.

Dan, Jack, and I were the only ones who couldn't get our weapons since the warriors had blocked off the street to my house, along with the street to Dan and Jack's houses, so we distracted the warriors while the others left. About forty minutes later when they returned Dan, Jack, and I tried getting our weapons again, but there was no way. I looked across the field when I noticed something strange over my house. It was a type of see-thru tunnel of fog leading from the sky onto the roof of my house. We managed to rush over to my house finally, but the tunnel was gone by the time we got there. Everything then faded to white, everyone was gone, and I was alone. All of a sudden I woke up in a cold sweat.

It was 4 a.m. and I couldn't fall back to sleep. This was really starting to bother me. Why was I having these dreams! This one was from the past, which had never happened before! I sat up on the edge of my bed in the darkness until I felt sleepy again, then I went back to bed. I slept calmly the rest of the night to where I didn't wake up until after nine later that morning. I spent the day cleaning my apartment, along with rearranging my furniture, until after dinner when I started calling Steve, Kevin, and Trevor. I told them that we needed to meet this coming Friday night, it was important. They agreed to my request then I called the kids' mom to ask if I could have them the following weekend. She said ok then let me go.

Afterward I sat down to watch some television and tried to relax until eventually I got tired so I went to bed. I spent the week job hunting during the day and restless nights with those same kinds of dreams until Friday finally came and I was anxious.

Steve, Kevin, and Trevor were set to arrive at 7 p.m. as I was picking up the kids at 6 p.m. I felt that it was time to reveal to them what had been happening to me. I tried to keep myself busy during the day in anticipation of the evening. Once I picked up the kids and got back to my apartment we goofed around until the others got there. Once they arrived we sat down in my living room where I told what had been happening to me with my bizarre dreams. They listened closely as I explained everything to them. When I was finished Steve asked me why I thought this was happening. I told him I had no explanation. They asked me what I wanted to do next. After thinking about it I said maybe we should take a trip into the time-zone, maybe we could find some answers there. They agreed so I activated the transporter, then once it was ready I energized it and we vanished.

Stage V ✦ ✦

Looking For Answers

We got to the fourth dimension then began looking for clues. I wasn't going to mention any of this to Phenom so we kept a low profile. After walking for awhile I wasn't seeing anything that gave me any answers so I thought maybe the answer wasn't here. We were about to start back to headquarters when Trevor suggested going to the sixth dimension. I quickly disagreed thinking that based on the information Phenom just gave me, it would be an unnecessary risk plus, given the apparent state of the energy warriors there it would be best to avoid contact with them. Steve and Kevin seemed to agree with me while Chrissy and Josh had no opinion, so we continued toward headquarters in order to go back to Earth. When we reached headquarters we checked our weapon supplies in the weapons chamber before transporting back to

Earth. A short time later we left the fourth dimension behind.

We got back to Earth about 10 p.m. as Steve, Kevin, and Trevor decided to spend the night as a precautionary measure. I arranged the living room to make accommodations for them then about 11 p.m. we decided to head to bed. Maybe due to the fact that I had my entire team over gave me some added comfort for that night I slept better than I had in a couple of weeks with no nightmares or strange dreams. The next day we hung out while we played Playstation and goofed around. If I didn't have the kids the guys and I would have gone out, but since we couldn't we went for a walk around dusk.

We walked down to end of my street where we stood watching the cars go by. We were just starting the head back up the street to go back to my apartment when Steve pointed out something above my apartment building. It was a transparent tunnel of fog coming from the sky onto the roof of my apartment building. This was impossible! I had only seen this once before long ago, but this couldn't possibly be happening!

"We have to get to my apartment now," I hollered as I started running down the street. The others looked confused but quickly started following me. I knew right away that someone was coming from the time-zone, but I didn't know who and I needed to find out immediately. I couldn't figure out how this was possible, this transporter hadn't been active long enough to be traced back to our universe. I was running so hard concentrating on the tunnel that I almost ran into a parked car on the street. As I got closer to my building the tunnel started to disappear, then by the time I got there the tunnel was gone. I stopped in front of the wishing well then hunched over to catch my breath while the others caught up to me a few moments later.

"Todd what is going on," Steve asked. "It's gone, where did it go," I asked. Where'd what go," Kevin asked. "The foggy tunnel!" "What are you talking about dad," Josh asked. "Didn't you guys see it? It was here and now it's gone!" "What tunnel? We didn't see anything dad, there's nothing here," Chrissy said. "Todd we haven't seen anything. We were down the street talking while watching cars go by when all of a sudden you hollered we had to go back to your apartment. You started running down the street hollering and flapping your arms in the air like a maniac," Kevin told me. "We turned around to try and figure out what you were doing and started chasing after you," Steve added. "You're messed up dude," Trevor mentioned. "Nothing ever happened over your apartment building," Steve pointed out. "Damn it I know what I saw!" "Let's go dad, maybe you just need to sit down," Chrissy said. As I started to calm down we began walking back up to my apartment.

Once we got upstairs I sat down on the Futon and tried to relax. Josh brought me some bottled water along with my cigarettes. After I lit up my cigarette I just sat there for a few minutes before I asked Trevor if he remembered that time when our old group was meeting in the church field by my old house. All of a sudden we looked over where we saw a see-thru tunnel of fog coming down from the sky onto the house. He said he remembered, but that was a long, long time ago. He then asked me if that's what

I thought I saw and I answered yes. Trevor would be the only one who would understand what I was talking about since, as you recall, he was part of my original team back in the 1980's and 1990's. He was there!

I took some time to explain to the others what had happened back then so they could understand what Trevor and I were talking about, but unless you were there you couldn't completely understand the whole concept. It was dark out at this point and none of us had eaten so we decided to go out and grab a bite. Later on when we got back to my place it was after 11 p.m. Everyone was staying the night again so we all went to bed. I closed my bedroom door, which I normally kept open, then set my alarm. I was planning a late night trip to the fourth dimension, alone.

A couple of hours later at 1:45 a.m. my alarm went off on my phone as I didn't set my main alarm since that was much louder plus, I didn't want to wake anyone else up. After seeing that everyone else was still sleeping, I crept back into my room, closed the door, and activated the transporter. A short time later I arrived at headquarters where I went to see Phenom. I wanted to see if he had attempted to transport to Earth. A short time later when I found him I asked him if he had tried coming to Earth and he answered no that they had not regained that ability. They could not survive on Earth for long periods of time, just as in the past.

He wanted to know why I was asking so I told him what had happened earlier that night back on Earth. He wasn't sure what to make of it, but he again reminded me that of how the energy warriors from the sixth dimension may possess that ability or perhaps I could have imagined it. In light of what had been happing with my lately with my bizarre dream he could easily be right. I knew there had to be an answer to all this somewhere, I wasn't going crazy. If no one here in the fourth dimension tried to cross over into my universe, then maybe someone else had tried, or maybe I really was going crazy. I couldn't find any answers here and perhaps I needed to look elsewhere. Maybe I did need to go to the sixth dimension, but it was extremely risky, especially alone. Part of me really wanted to go investigate the sixth dimension; however, in the end I decided to forego that option so I returned to Earth.

When I arrived home it was 1:45 a.m. the same time as when I had left. After I got into my pajamas I sat in bed for awhile then finally went to bed. I slept in the next morning as we all got up around 9 a.m. I made pancakes, bacon, hash browns, and toast for everyone. Later on just after lunch we headed for the mall where we stayed for a couple of hours just walking around and window shopping. After the mall I decided to take everyone over by my old house. Once we got to my old neighborhood we parked our cars and got out. I took them on a tour of my old "turf" showing them my old house, as well as the field. We walked over by where we held that meeting the night that the tunnel appeared so they could get a visual perspective of how it was that night. We spent a few hours walking around looking into my past then we headed back to my apartment.

Stage VI ⋆ ✦

Unexpected Visitor

We grabbed something to eat, sat around for a little bit, then about 8 p.m. Steve, Kevin, and Trevor were getting ready to leave. Just as they were walking out the door we heard a noise coming from my room. They stopped in the doorway for a moment then stepped back inside. "What was that noise," Steve asked. "I heard it too," Kevin said. "Yeah me too," Trevor added. "Let's find out," Chrissy said. "Alright, but cautiously," I answered as Josh decided to hide in my coat closet while the rest of us walked slowly toward my room in silence.

When we got to my room in my closet there was a glow coming from the other side of the door. I glanced at the control panel and saw that the transporter had been activated. The only way this could have happened was if someone had tried, or was trying to transport here. I had proof now, along with witnesses, that I wasn't going crazy. Just then the power went out in my apartment, all except the control panel which ran on a separate power source. "What the hell," Kevin said softly. "What happened dad," Chrissy whispered. "Aw crap," Steve mumbled. "Shh, everyone grab your weapons, hurry," I said. Everyone scattered to quickly get their weapons then we all took positions anticipating someone arriving.

Kevin and Trevor crouched down on the far side of my bed directly across from the closet door while Chrissy wrapped herself around her bedroom doorway right next to my room. I ducked into the bathroom doorway directly across from Chrissy and Steve put his back to the wall of my dining room where he could peek his head around the corner as everyone was focused on my room. Josh finally came out of the coat closet where he crouched down in the archway between the kitchen and the foyer by the front door. We waited for something to happen, someone to come through the door, but nothing happened, no one came through. We were starting to let our guard down when we heard another noise.

We tightened up our stance as we waited once again in anticipation. The transporter was cycling, meaning someone was coming, so we waited with our weapons drawn until the cycle finished. Once the cycle was complete the power in the apartment came back on. The glow inside the closet dimmed, then the door began to open and to our surprise, as well as relief, it was Turion. I called out to him, "Turion, Turion is that you?" He answered back confirming it was him so I signaled the team to stand down. I asked Turion what he was doing here and how.

He told me that Phenom had sent him here to warn us that Denon, with his warriors, were planning something and that they may be possibly be coming to Earth. "Ok that answers the why, but what about the how?" Turion explained that they had regained the ability to travel once again in their own universe so they were able to once again travel anywhere. Phenom, Athlon, Duron, as well as Turion himself, had been working nonstop after my last visit to find the right frequency to trace my transporter signal. Once they finally found the right frequency and traced the signal, Phenom had sent him to warn us about the possible threat.

The other thing that Turion wanted to inform us was that Phenom had begun working with modulating their energy flow to allow them to better adapt to our universe, or at least allow them to stay here on Earth longer than before. If Denon were to discover, or already possessed that ability to adapt in our universe, then the threat to Earth was very real. According to Turion, Phenom also felt that it was only a matter of time before Denon would find the frequency to get to Earth.

This information that Turion had brought us was crucial, so I deeply thanked him then asked if he wanted to stay. He said that he wished that he could, but they hadn't perfected the modulation of energy yet so he had to get back. I told him that I understood as I thanked him again and told him to please pass along our gratitude to Phenom, as well as the others. He promised that he would then transported back to the fourth dimension. "Todd, we've got a problem," Steve said. "A BIG problem," Trevor added. "Yes we do," I answered. "Dad I'm scared," Chrissy said. "You should be Chrissy, we all should be." Josh started to whimper, then ran back inside to coat closet.

Stage VII

Our next Move

The rest of us made our way to the living room and sat down. We sat there a few minutes not saying a word until Steve broke the silence. "So Todd what do we do?" "I can think of only two possibilities Steve, either we go to the sixth dimension, or we at least go into the time-zone and stay in there." "Are you nuts," Kevin yelled. "Why would we want to do that Todd," Trevor asked. "It's the only thing I can think of Trevor, go into the time-zone so we can stop time. This isn't like when we were kids Trevor, we're all grown up and scattered through five states. My biggest fear is that Denon, with his warriors, will find their way to Earth and strike when we are all separated. If that happened it is doubtful that we would reunite all of us in time to fight them off.

"That is a valid point," Steve said in agreement then added, "I recommend we go to the fourth dimension to plan our strategy from there, at least we'll stop time in the process." The others agreed so I went to drag Josh out of the coat closet while Steve set the coordinates. A few moments later we transported and the clock had stopped. We arrived at headquarters then began checking our weapons and made sure we had an ample supply in our weapons chamber. We also armed ourselves with energy rifles then began discussing a strategy, or different strategies. We stayed in headquarters for awhile trying to figure out what our next move should be. We reached an impasse plus, it was late so we broke discussions for the night and began re-energizing. Some time later when we finished and regained consciousness, we stayed in headquarters briefly before exiting out into the corridor.

We decided to do some walking for a change of scenery then returned to headquarters later on. We resumed our discussion trying to determine our next move, then during our discussion we got an incoming message from Phenom. I hadn't mentioned it before but recently Turion, along with me, had adapted our headquarters in order to communicate directly with Phenom, as well as Athlon in the city. Something else to pass along that I have never mentioned is how time is measured in the fourth dimension. They have an equivalent twenty-four hour day like our own and it divided into thirds which they call Phases. Before I have always used an Earth translation to describe morning, afternoon, and evening; however, the actual depiction would be morning, Phase I, afternoon, Phase II, and evening, Phase III.

Returning to Phenom, he informed me that he had detected our arrival during Phase III of the previous day and he wished to meet with us, so he asked us to come to the city. I agreed, ended communications, and we left headquarters. A short time later when we arrived in the city we met up with Phenom. He told us that there was no new information for us, but he asked if we were planning on going to the sixth dimension. I told him that we had considered the possibility, but we hadn't determined our next course of action yet.

He then brought something to my attention the never crossed our minds. If Denon discovered our frequency and obtained the ability to travel to our universe, they could travel directly to Earth from the sixth dimension. In that case if were here in the fourth dimension Denon and his warriors could reach Earth without our knowledge. We had to make another decision, do we stay here in the fourth dimension to keep time from moving, or head back to Earth where we would be forced to be separated. There was no guarantee that they would come to Earth, but if we stayed here and they did we would not be there to stop them. I went around the group to get everyone's input before I made the tough decision for us to return to Earth. We had to continue our normal routine back home.

If they were to come to our world at least we would be there to know about it, most likely I would be the first one to know. Phenom told us he would try to monitor their activities from here and if anything new developed he would signal for me and I could transport directly to the city. I agreed then concluded our discussion. Afterwards we returned to headquarters to check things out before returning to Earth. Some time later when we finished up at headquarters it was near the end of Phase II.

We transported back to Earth and it was about 8:30 p.m. when we arrived. Steve, Kevin, and Trevor had to leave so they could get back to their everyday lives while I had to take Josh and Chrissy back home. On our way out Steve asked me what would happen if Denon and his warriors came to Earth while everybody was scattered about. I told him I would cross that bridge if we came to it. When we got downstairs to the parking lot we went our separate ways with the understanding that I would be in contact with them more than usual. I dropped the kids off then returned home as it was almost 10 p.m.

Stage VIII ✦ ✦

New Addition

I was alone now and would be the first and the only to know if Denon reached Earth. I sat down in the living room for awhile thinking, then after contemplating an idea for some time I decided that tomorrow I was going to do something that I had not intended on. About 11 p.m. I went to bed hoping to get some sleep. The following morning I woke up feeling well rested as surprisingly I had gotten a good night sleep. I grabbed some coffee like usual then around 11 a.m. I got dressed for the day.

I checked the control panel, but there was no signal from Phenom, which meant that nothing had changed, at least anything that he knew about. I went downstairs to the parking lot to check and see if my neighbor's car was there. It was so I went back upstairs. I knocked on my neighbor's door, which was diagonal from mine. A few minutes later he answered the door. His name was Tom, he was just two years younger than me and we had become pretty good friends over the last couple of years. I asked him if he was busy and in telling me no I invited him over to my place. We made some small talk for a little while before I brought up the point of why I asked him over.

I very slowly and calmly began explaining everything to him, everything from 1988 until now. I took my time revealing everything to him so I wouldn't overload Tom with too much information. The conversation lasted over three hours, with many questions from Tom, but by the time I was finished he expressed an interest. It was time for the next stage; I invited him to go on a little trip with me. He was a little reluctant at first but then he agreed to go. I took him to my room where I showed him my closet, along with the control panel, as he seemed skeptical until I activated the transporter.

At that point he took a much greater interest as he kept asking me if we were really going to disappear by standing in a walk-in closet. He paced around a little as he kept looking at the closet door as well as the control panel. A few minutes later when the transporter was ready I opened the door and invited him to step inside. He hesitated at first then cautiously took a step in as he looked around. He asked me what that glow was so I explained that it was the energy which would allow us to transport.

Tom took a few more small steps until he was all the way in the closet before he turned around to face my bedroom. A few moments after that I set the coordinates, energized the transporter, and stepped in the closet where I stood next to Tom then we vanished. We arrived at headquarters, then as we stepped out of the transporter Tom began looking around the room and was stunned. I started explaining everything to him so he could absorb his surroundings to stay calm.

After I gave him a tour of headquarters explaining what everything was, as well as what we were in this world. I energized the door and we stepped out into the corridor. We spent Phase II as well as part of Phase III walking around while I gave him a tour of the place along with identifying what everything was. At one point we ran into some warriors and he freaked out. I managed to calm him down, then after awhile he thought it was pretty sweet here. We eventually made our way back top headquarters, then we transported back to Earth. It was 2:15 p.m. when we returned and once Tom saw my clocks he thought they were broken.

He immediately went back to his place to check his clocks but they had the same time on them. He then ran back to my place and asked how that was possible so I explained how that worked the best I could since I never really figured that out myself in which afterward he understood a little better.

He stayed as we talked some more while I tried to answer any further questions he had, then Tom left at 3 p.m. Tom had accepted my offer in joining the team and was officially our newest member. Let me take a few moments to explain my actions. It was a difficult decision getting someone else involved in this time-zone business, but I felt that the situation warranted it. Tom was very close, he was right there compared to everyone else and I needed someone close just in case. Tom was also very handy as he worked on cars in his spare time and he also used to do maintenance here at our apartment complex. His skills would make him an excellent addition to the team.

Later on after dinner I called Steve, Kevin, and Trevor to let them know about Tom. I mentioned that they could meet him the next time came over this upcoming weekend. Josh and Chrissy already knew Tom since they occasionally played with his son Mason when they were over so I didn't call them. They could be informed of his addition as a team member the next time they came over. By the time I finished calling everyone it was 9:30 p.m. so I sat down to watch television as I tried to clear my head. The rest of the week went by pretty quiet plus, there was no new information from Phenom.

Stage IX ⸴

A Step Back In Time

The end of the week had come and late afternoon on Friday I was driving around, specifically on the main road near my old neighborhood. I happened to look in the direction of my old house where I clearly saw that tunnel of fog over the house. I concentrated on it so hard trying to determine it was really there that I almost went off the road so I pulled over to get out of my car. I stared over at the house for thirty seconds or so, rubbing my eyes and blinking to make sure it was there and when it didn't go away I started to panic. I got back into the car, peeled out, then sharply turned onto a street that led to my old subdivision as I was headed for the house. It was as if Denon had found a different frequency and had activated the original transporter, but that was impossible since that transporter had been destroyed by the Eclipse team years ago.

If that transporter had somehow been reactivated then we had a new set of problems. This would mean that for the first time there was more than one doorway to and from the time-zone, plus Denon with his warriors could possibly arrive from two locations. I got to the end of my old street then came to a screeching halt. I got out of the car then just stood there looking down the street at my old house. The foggy tunnel remained so I made my way over to the sidewalk on the opposite side of my old house. Once I was down the street I stopped directly across from the house where I used to live and stared at the tunnel. It was apparent that it was real and not an illusion so the next thing I needed to figure out was how long it had been there, as well as if they were already here.

I grabbed my cell phone and immediately called Steve to let him know what was going on. He recommended that I contact the others then he said that he would leave momentarily to meet up with me. I called Kevin and Trevor but I couldn't get a hold of them so I left an urgent voicemail with each of them. I looked back in the direction of where my apartment was but saw nothing in the sky. At least that area was safe for the moment, but then I realized that I had no weapons and if they were here I was defenseless. My apartment was no more than a five minute drive from here so I could go back to arm myself, but I didn't know if I should leave or not.

I had to know if they were here so I did something that was either very daring or very stupid. I walked across the street then walked up the driveway. I came up to the front porch where I stood in front of the door, then after a moment I rang the doorbell. I stood and waited but no one answered, then I noticed that the front door was cracked open. I checked the screen door and it was unlocked so I slowly opened the screen door where I peeked through the small opening into the family room.

I hollered to see if anyone was home as I slowly pushed the front door open. The house was quiet so I took one step inside as I continued to call out to see if anyone was there. I smelled something funny, something that had a horrible odor. I peered around the front door into the foyer off to my left and saw a body lying there. Whoever it was, perhaps the owner, was dead. I then became very quiet assuming that Denon had done this. Instead of heading toward the kitchen I quietly made my way through the family room to the hallway where all the bedrooms were.

I peeked around the wall looking down the hallway toward my old room. I crouched down and crawled down the hallway to a small bedroom on the right and ducked in there. I stayed low and peered around the doorway to look down the hallway again. There was a bathroom on the right and my old room was straight ahead. I listened closely for a moment, listening for a generating sound form the other bathroom in the bedroom, listening for anything out of the ordinary but all that could be heard was silence.

I slowly crawled back out into the hallway and carefully made my way to the main bathroom. Once I reached it I crawled inside the doorway. I stopped and took a moment to try and slow my breathing. I carefully looked around the corner as my old bedroom door was just a few feet away. I began inching my way out of the bathroom as I had one hand and knee out in the hallway carpet when I began hearing a generating sound. The sound was coming from the other bathroom off my old bedroom. "They're coming," I said softly to myself and froze up. I just stayed there not moving with myself still half in the main bathroom and half out.

I needed to do something quick or at least move as I was exposed and vulnerable. I then made my move and I quickly scurried from the main bathroom into my old bedroom and ducked into the closet. The closet was just inside the bedroom doorway to the left and opposite where the doorway was to the small bathroom which allowed me to see the whole room as I kept the closet door opened just a crack. I stood there in the closet as quietly as I could while my heart pounded in my chest. I started to see a glow emanating from inside the bathroom. They would be here any moment and I had no way to stop them.

I then heard a sound which resembled an activated transporter. A few moments later the glow faded and it got quiet again, then I heard voices coming from the bathroom. Shortly afterward I began hearing footsteps and as they entered the room I could see them. There were four of them and I could pick out which one of them was Denon. He was telling the others that this facility had been secured and they would set up base here while the others arrived. He said that he had determined the approximate location of the Earth beings and they would wait until the rest of the squadron arrived before they would begin their advancement.

They were exiting the bedroom headed toward the kitchen when my cell phone started ringing. "Shit," I blurted out in a loud whisper as I tried to quiet my phone.

They stopped a few steps into the kitchen and listened for the source of the sudden sound. "What was that," I heard Denon say to the others. "Apparently we are not alone. Search the area and find the source of that noise," he instructed the others. They began to fan out as two of them headed toward the foyer that led to the family room and another came back into the hallway and started heading down the hallway toward the other bedrooms. After standing in the kitchen a few moments Denon re-entered my old bedroom and began looking around.

I was trapped and if he opened the closet door I would be discovered. If he came far enough into the room and would head towards the bathroom I could attempt to escape. He stood in the doorway and looked around. Fortunately he started slowly walking toward the bathroom. As he did I thrust open the closet door and dashed out of the bedroom and into the kitchen. I quickly turned right and ran into the attached dining room area to the sliding glass door. I hurried up and opened the sliding glass door and struggled to open the sliding screen door. By this time Denon had ran back into the kitchen, turned toward the dining and saw me. "Stop human," he hollered. "Warriors out here," he echoed and began to pursue me. I managed to finally open the sliding screen door and jumped into the backyard. I came to the privacy fence gate and struggled with that. Denon and the other warriors made their way onto the patio just as I managed to get the gate open.

He hollered again for me to stop and I quickly closed the gate and locked it while keeping the key. I aimed for the church field and started running as fast as I could.

While running through the field I got my phone out and voice dialed Steve. It turned out that he was the one who called me when I was hiding in the closet. When he answered I hollered, "Where are you?" He said he was in my apartment parking lot. Then it hit me, I left my damn car parked at the end of my old street! I couldn't turn around and go back because I would have to pass in front of my old house in order to get to it and Denon with the others were standing on the driveway and could see the direction I was headed in.

"Steve get to the church now and pick me up," I hollered into the phone. "What? What are you doing there," he asked. "No time to explain just get here now!" "On my way Todd, ETA four minutes." I hung up the phone and continued running. I was almost to the church parking lot. Denon had sent two warriors to pursue me while he and the third warrior stayed behind watching from the driveway. The two warriors pursuing me had just hit the field so I had a decent head start. I was going to cut through the parking lot and head down one of the long driveways that led to the main road where I could rendezvous with Steve. I just hit the church parking lot and was ready to collapse but I managed to keep running. Unfortunately I no longer had my prime physique I once had in my youth. If Steve did not get here soon I was either going to fall over or get captured, or fall over then get captured.

I was approaching the driveway and could see Steve turning in off the main road at the other end. I started waving my arms to get his attention and looked behind me to check the distance between myself and the warriors. They were halfway across the field so I still had the advantage for the moment until they started firing at me. Steve started up the driveway until I caught up with him almost halfway. He stopped his van and I quickly got in. "What in the world is going on," he asked. I started explaining what was happening in between breaths, where I had been and what I had discovered. I asked him to double back so I could retrieve my car. He said ok and circled around the side streets to get back. Once we got back to my car I could see Denon and that warrior still standing on the driveway so I pointed them out to Steve.

The two warriors that were chasing me were coming back through the field towards the house. As I got out of the van I told Steve to wait then follow me back to my apartment. He acknowledged and waited as I made my way toward my car. I was fortunate that Denon and the others had not seen me as I got in. I quickly backed up then peeled out while Steve began to follow. For the moment it seemed we had escaped the situation. We made our way out of the subdivision and back to the main road. Once we reached the main road I looked in the direction of my apartment looking up toward the sky checking for a foggy tunnel. Nothing was there which gave me some relief. A few minutes later we arrived at my apartment and quickly ran upstairs.

As soon as we stepped inside the doorway I quickly slammed the door shut and locked it. Steve looked at me for a moment while I was breathing out of control. I took a minute to calm down so I could explain to him what was going on. I told him everything that happened, how I was on the main road and happened to see the foggy tunnel over my old house. I had decided to go investigate and how

I crept down my old street, how I walked up the driveway, how the front door was cracked open, how I entered and found the dead body in the foyer and how I crept my way into my old bedroom where I first saw them arrive.

I then told Steve what I had overheard, how they were planning on coming after us and they were certain on my location. I said to him that I was reasonably confident that we were safe for the moment. I speculated that Denon wouldn't make any advancement until his squadron had arrived. He asked me how long I thought we had and I answered saying probably not long and that they were most likely on their way as we speak. Steve got a very concerned look on his face which I shared. "This is exactly what I was afraid of, them arriving when the team was separated," Steve said. "Yes that's exactly right," I answered. I told Steve that we had very little time and we needed to get a hold of the others. We would need everyone on the team if we were to have a chance. Steve agreed and asked if I had any ideas.

I told him to hold that thought. I called my ex and asked if it was alright if I took the kids for awhile. She said that was fine and asked when I wanted them. I told her now and asked if it was alright if Steve picked them up since I was a little tied up at the moment. She agreed and before she hung up I told her to make sure kids had their "weekend kits," which was our code word for their weapons. After I hung up I asked Steve to go pick up the kids and I would attempt to contact Kevin and Trevor. While I stayed behind I could monitor the transporter here at the apartment for any activity and keep watch for approaching enemy warriors.

He understood and quickly left. As soon as he did I bolted up the front door and went to my room to make my calls. While in my room I could get a better view of the street and there was only one direction the warriors could approach from. After a few attempts I was able to reach Kevin. I informed him of our situation and the urgency for him to rendezvous with Steve and I as soon as possible. He said he had something going on with his wife and daughter and would try to get here as soon as he could. I then contacted Trevor and got a hold of him right away. I told him the same thing I told Kevin and by the time I hung up the phone he was already in his car and on his way. I started pacing around my room and kept looking out my east bedroom window. The east window faced the length of the street allowing me to look all the way down to the end of it where they would enter from.

Trying to stay calm I occasionally looked at the control panel checking for any activity and going to the front door double-checking the locks, as well as peeking out the front window down toward the circle and wishing well before going back to my room starting the cycle all over again. I had completely lost track of time and eventually, almost an hour later, I saw Steve coming down the street. Now that he was back with Josh and Chrissy all we were missing was Kevin and Trevor. A few minutes later Steve, Josh, and Chrissy were in my apartment. Steve told me that he had tried to explain to them what was going on so I filed in the gaps.

Stage X ✦ ✦

Taking Position

The kids immediately unpacked and got their weapons ready. Josh and Chrissy went into her room while Steve stayed in the living room guarding the front door and watching the wishing well area. I remained in my room standing watch over the rest of the street through my two bedroom windows as well as guarding the transporter. About forty-five minutes later Trevor showed up so we just needed Kevin, but I had no way of knowing when he would be here. It was after 8 p.m. and dark outside making it harder to see them if they approached. When Trevor got inside he came into my room so I could further explain to him what was happening while I kept watch. About 8:30 p.m. Kevin called saying he had finally been able to get away and he would be here in a couple of hours. At least he was on his way and hopefully he would get here before anything happened.

We remained in lockdown in my apartment as the tension continued to mount with each passing minute. Trevor took my place as I took a brief break to get something to eat. All of us periodically rotated giving everyone a chance to eat or take care of any personal needs. It was decided that we would have someone on watch constantly. Trevor volunteered to stand watch overnight while we tried to sleep. A twenty-four hour watch seemed prudent for the situation and the decision was unanimous. Finally about 10:45 p.m. Kevin arrived. Josh and Chrissy had gone to bed shortly before Kevin showed up. Trevor stood watch in my room and Steve by the front door while I sat down with Kevin in the living room and explained what was going on.

After I finished explaining, Steve, Kevin, and I went to bed while Trevor remained up in the living room for the start of the night watch. I woke up the next morning at 7 a.m. my usual time. When I got to the living room Trevor was sitting on the Futon quietly watching T.V. and had kept the curtains in the living room open all night to keep an eye on the street below. I grabbed some coffee and joined him on the Futon and we quietly talked while the others slept. About an hour later Steve had woke up shortly followed by Kevin and they joined us. About 9 a.m. Trevor slipped out to my room to go to sleep while the kids were just waking up. We all sat in the living room talking and relieved that the night had passed without incident. The kids played on the PS2 while the three of us sat around talking and drinking our coffee while Kevin and I smoked our cigarettes.

About 10 a.m. I started making breakfast. Everyone wanted my famous pancakes and hash browns, along with bacon, sausage, and toast as I spared no expense. I admit we let our guard down for most of the morning so after we ate we got ready for the day and began rotating our watch from the living room. The day had been a quiet one and Trevor woke up around 3 p.m. He came out and helped himself to the fridge while I stepped into my room and began looking out through the east window. As I did the day before I occasionally checked the transporter control panel for any signals from Phenom. About 5:30 p.m. we ordered pizza and had it delivered as we could not afford to leave the apartment at this time.

After Dinner Steve came to me with a suggestion. His idea was to have a team go and check my old house to see if the tunnel was still there and if possible determine the position of Denon's squadron. It was too risky, I wasn't comfortable splitting up the team, especially on Earth and I had to reject his proposal. He reminded me that as adults we had the luxury of driving so we could easily outrun them, something I couldn't have done years ago. I reminded him that he couldn't fully understand how powerless we were on Earth compared to the time-zone. Despite our weapons and combined efforts there was a very good chance that we would not succeed. He argued that he'd rather know in advance if they were headed this way. I fell silent as Steve had made a valid point I suppose so against my better judgment I allowed him to go.

It was decided that Kevin and Trevor would join Steve while I stayed behind with Josh and Christina. I stressed to Steve to make sure all their cell phones were fully charged and to keep in regular contact with me. Steve agreed and they left shortly afterwards. With the three of them gone it did create more elbow room in my apartment. It was early afternoon by this time and nothing had changed. I had just spoken with Steve and he told me that they had made a circle through my old subdivision passing my old street and that tunnel of fog was still there. He also told me that they had taken position in the corner of the church parking lot to get a fix on Denon and his squadron.

I acknowledged and told him that I wanted updates every thirty minutes or if anything suddenly changed. We hung up and I went to the living room to sit down where I stopped to think for a moment. *What would we do once they start to advance? Do we go to the house and try to keep them from advancing, or do we wait and have them come to us. If they do come here to the apartment do we run to the fourth dimension or should we go to the field behind the church and make our stand there?* I guess I really needed to think about what our best option was. Until now I thought that barricading ourselves here was best, but I was reconsidering what the best course of action was. It was hard to concentrate as I was beginning to fell cooped up.

I started paying closer attention to Josh and Christina to look for signs of boredom, unhappiness, or any other signs that were negative. Part of the reason I wanted to stay here was to monitor the transporter for any activity or in case Phenom tried to contact me. I was also aware that everyone else would want to get out of here to avoid feeling locked up. I myself was content to stay here for I often would not leave my place for long periods of time, almost like being a hermit. I gave my mind a brief rest by grabbing a snack from the kitchen and sitting down at the dining room table. As far as the kids were concerned I was more worried about Christina than I was Josh. Christina tended to get bored more easily and there wasn't much to do here where as Josh was content to stay in the apartment sitting around all day playing PS2.

It was almost 3 p.m. and Steve called to report in. They were still in the church parking lot conducting their surveillance. He informed that they were starting to see some activity and asked for further instructions. I asked him to specify and he told me that Denon had come out to the driveway along with twenty or so warriors. He also said that the tunnel remained over the house. He believed that warriors were still transporting here from the sixth dimension and hypothesized that possibly a great number warriors were already here and in the house. Based on that information I immediately ruled out the church field option as there was little protection and we would be out in the open and completely exposed.

With the Blitz team currently split up and determining that we would be at an extreme disadvantage by storming into my old house in any type of raid, I concluded that we would have to make our stand here at my apartment. Steve had taken an ideal position in that he was parked in the corner of the church parking lot at the edge of the far driveway while the van face toward the main road allowing for a quick departure if needed. All of them were monitoring the house from the back of the van peering out from the tailgate window.

After wrestling the idea for a time I reached a difficult and potentially risky decision. I told Steve to leave Kevin and Trevor there to continue their surveillance and return here long enough to pick up Christina. I thought she might want to escape from the confines of my apartment for awhile. I believed that Kevin and Trevor would be alright there with no transportation for a short period of time. They could position themselves around the corner of the church building where they could peer around the corner without being seen. If anything changed they were to contact me immediately. Trevor's experience would allow them to handle the situation if needed. Steve wouldn't be gone more than ten minutes so I felt they would be fine.

While waiting for Steve to return I unlocked my front door long enough to walk across the hall to go get Tom. He was finally home and available so I had him come over. Once we returned to my place we took a seat in the living room and I filled him in on what was going on. While explaining everything to him Steve returned long enough to pick up Christina. Tom left long enough to go back to his place and grab his cigarettes then returned to join me and Josh. Steve contacted me once he returned to the church parking lot retaking his previous position. He told me that Trevor reported to him there had been no change.

It was going on 4 p.m. now. I asked Steve how long they planned on staying there and he answered by saying all of them agreed to stay two to three hours. I let it go and said alright. I hung up with Steve and went back to talking with Tom. He had more questions for me which I gladly took time to try to answer. After talking for awhile it was getting close to dinner. Tom offered to run and bring back some fast food for us so I could watch and monitor the transporter. I gladly accepted but the cardinal rule applied, "You fly, I buy." After Tom took off I checked the transporter control panel and the signal from Phenom had been activated. I wondered if he had information for me since I had not gone and told him that Denon was on Earth. I checked on Josh and he was in a zone playing a game so I decided to go see Phenom and besides no one would even know I was gone.

I had to stop and think about that for a moment I had never gone into the time-zone when warriors were here on Earth so I didn't know if time would still stop. I decided to wait until after dinner just in case it didn't for two reasons. The first reason was I didn't want Josh alone. It wasn't because of his age, after all he was 15 years old now, but in case Denon came. I didn't want Tom coming back and wondering where the hell I went if time didn't stop. The second reason was I didn't want to lose out on any of my food. I waited and about fifteen minutes later Tom returned with the food. It was Taco Bell night for me and I didn't waste any time digging in. While waiting I told Tom about the signal I had got from Phenom.

Stage XI ✦ ✦

Preparations

After dinner Tom was going to stay with Josh and I also had him and Steve exchange phone numbers. I was off to pay Phenom a very brief visit to see what he wanted. I started energizing the transporter and told Tom the place was his until I returned. Once it was ready I stepped in the transporter and vanished. I transported directly to the city and quickly sought out Phenom. I found Athlon and she had Turion take me to him. My time there was brief but I managed to find out what Phenom wanted. He believed that Denon was mounting large numbers of troops for a possible invasion of Earth and possibly the fourth dimension as well. I told him I was aware of the situation on Earth since Denon was already there. Phenom was unaware of this just as I was unaware of any immediate threat to the fourth dimension. The information we exchanged proved very beneficial to both of us.

I obviously couldn't be in two places at once. It was decided that Phenom and I would keep in contact with one another. He said he was ready to defend the fourth dimension and they were on full alert. He would continue to watch over things here while I dealt with the situation on Earth. He would signal me again if the situation here changed. We concluded our discussion and Turion escorted me back to the transporter. Along the way he and I talked more about the situation. Once we arrived at the transporter we went our separate ways wishing each other success and I vanished back to Earth.

When I returned the first thing I did was check to see if time had stopped. The answer was no that time had not stopped and I believed I knew why. I went into the living room where Tom and Josh were. Tom said, "Hey you've been gone awhile. I thought you said that time stopped or something when we went there." "How long, wait I know…. I've been gone for over three hours," I said. Tom told me that Steve and the others would be back any minute.

I mentioned that I believed I knew why time hadn't stopped. I wanted to wait until the others arrived so I could express my theory to everyone. At that time they returned and knocked our prearranged code on the door so I knew it was them. After they got inside and the front door was resealed we all went into the living room. I explained to them what had just happened and my thoughts as to the reason why. Steve said that they knew I was gone. He had checked in with Tom twice and discovered I was not around.

I explained why I believed the reason time did not stop this last time I went to the fourth dimension. I felt it was because the warriors from the sixth dimension were here and that they were still transporting to Earth. The other possibility was that the foggy tunnel that was over my old house was causing the doorway to remain open, or both. With the doorway open it somehow affected time from stopping. The more I thought about it the more I believed it had to do with the foggy tunnel keeping the doorway open. I called for everyone's opinion, particularly Steve's due to his knowledge of science and science fiction. He seemed to agree that the foggy tunnel somehow caused the doorway to remain open and thus preventing time from stopping if we left Earth.

Something else had just occurred to me. This was the first time that there were two transporters here on Earth. I did not know what kind of effect this would have on either transporter if any, or our traveling from Earth to the time-zone. Again I didn't know if there was any significance to that but it was something to be aware of. It was going on 11 p.m. and it had been a long and stressful day. Rest seemed to be in order so we prepared for bed. Trevor would again take the night watch and settled in the living room. The rest of us said goodnight and headed for the bedrooms. When I climbed into bed I laid there and started thinking if we were taking the right approach. Were we better off going after them at my old house or letting them come to us? I just wasn't sure anymore.

The next morning my alarm started blaring. "Shit it's already 7 a.m.," I mumbled. I stumbled out of bed then went over and slapped my alarm clock off. I threw on my sweatshirt and sweatpants and stumbled to the kitchen to get my coffee. I made my way into the living room saying good morning to Trevor who was quietly watching TV. He reported no incidents during the night.

He was tired so by 7:30 a.m. he went to bed. Steve and Kevin got up by 8 a.m. and the kids were up by 9 a.m. Tom had returned home last night and had to work today so he wouldn't be available until this afternoon. For a change in the menu selection Steve and I went to go get McDonald's for breakfast and brought it back for everyone. While eating we discussed our strategy for the day.

Today everyone except me would go stake out my old house. Even if he was content to stay here I felt that Josh needed some fresh air. He was even more of a homebody than I was. If anything happened here I would have Trevor to assist me. After breakfast we got ready for the day and around 11 a.m. Steve and the others left. I quietly stayed in the living room so I wouldn't disturb Trevor. Once they got there Steve contacted me to inform me that they were in position. He also said that the foggy tunnel remained over my old house.

I told him to touch base every hour or if the situation changed. After we finished speaking I listened to the TV as I started thinking if we were going about this the right way. I was fully aware that everyone would have to get back to their lives eventually despite the situation at hand. With time not stopping here on Earth if they did not get home by the end of the weekend our secret would be exposed. Despite my efforts I still didn't think that everyone fully understood just how vulnerable we were on Earth. The incident we had faced in the twelfth dimension was a walk in the park compared to this.

This had to stop. The cycle must end here and now. I was just about to call Steve to tell him after Tom got home the three of us would join them and we would penetrate their Earth base. It was 2 p.m. and Tom would be home around 3:30 p.m. Steve told me don't bother as he was just about to contact me to inform me that the warriors were on the move. I asked him how large their forces were and he replied it was massive, it looked like hundreds. "Hundreds! It's an all out invasion," I hollered. "We don't have a chance Steve, no chance! You'd better get back here now," I said to him. He agreed and stayed on the line as they started back. He said that they were taking the main route, the most direct route to the apartment.

Steve made a point to return quickly and about five minutes later they were back. I let them in then went and woke Trevor up. He stumbled out to the living room and we explained what was going on. I did run across the hall to leave a note on Tom's door to meet up with us as soon as he could. When I got back I ran into my bedroom and activated the control panel and signaled Phenom.

I remained in my room staring out of the east window. That would be the direction they would be coming from. Steve entered my room to talk. Everyone else was getting their weapons ready. Again I asked Steve if he was certain that many were coming. He answered that he was certain and he had not exaggerated. I rubbed my head while thinking as I often did and eventually told Steve that I was considering contacting Gannon for assistance from the Eclipse Team.

Steve agreed and strongly urged me to do so. If the warriors were walking at a normal pace it would take them twenty to thirty minutes to reach us. Steve pointed out our lack of time and recommended that if I were going to contact Gannon I should do so immediately. "I have no choice but to contact Phenom. Go quickly and bring the others in here for a moment," I told Steve. He quickly exited my room and brought the others back. When they entered my room I had them sit down on my bed. "What's going on dad?" Chrissy asked. "I need to tell you all something so you are fully aware of our situation," I said. They all glued their eyes on me focused on what I had to tell them as I began to explain.

"I learned something long time ago when the energy warriors first came to Earth during our war with them. The weapons we take into the time-zone have no effect or special powers here on Earth, they are just ordinary things. As Trevor would know, back then we used very different weapons and what we took into the time-zone became unique and more of a weapon, just like now. For example I used a mini blowtorch, which was nothing more than a lighter and a can of hairspray, but in the time-zone it was a much different and more powerful weapon. Now what we take into the time-zone takes a more dramatic transformation. For instance, Chrissy your weapons in the time-zone are basically useless here. Your water pick is just a water pick, not a cutting beam. Your rubber bands are useless and no energy bolts come from your braces. The only thing useful for us here on Earth would be your magnetic darts."

"So I take it my MP3 player is only good for listening to music?" Kevin asked. "And my processors are only good in a computer?" Steve asked. "I'm afraid so." "How are we supposed to defend ourselves this time?" Trevor asked. "I do have one solution, something I remembered from the last time we faced a similar situation. One thing that is not affected for some reason would be the energy rifles. We can arm ourselves with energy rifles and will be able to defend ourselves," I said. "Whatever we do we better do it quick Todd, they'll be here anytime," Steve said. He was right we had to act now before we ran out of time. Just then the transporter became active, someone was coming. We all scattered just as we had before.

The cycle finished and the door opened as and Phenom, along with Turion, stood before me. They had received my signal and were just now responding. I told them that there was no time to waste and Denon with his warriors would be here any minute. I did ask them two things though. First, we needed weapons since we had nothing of real use here on here on Earth, so I asked if they could provide any. Second, if they could assist us in any way because we were heavily outnumbered. Phenom looked at Turion then looked back at me.

Phenom replied, "I will send Turion to bring you back weapons. I will stay here until he returns. As for your second request; do you remember that last time I was here I told you that we had not found a solution and could not remain on Earth for more than fifteen of your minutes? What if I told you we have overcome that difficulty?" "How," I asked.

"Something we should have tried sooner. Turion hurry, go and bring back weapons for our allies and four squadrons. Put three more on stand-by and return quickly." "Right away Phenom," Turion answered. The transporter was activated and Turion vanished. Once Turion was gone Phenom resumed his explanation. "Duron gave me a suggestion. Duron mentioned how he and Sempron were able to travel to the twelfth dimension to assist you against the ice warriors. We began to experiment modifying our energy flow just as Sempron and Duron had done before. The challenge for us was more difficult this time since we have to cross over into your universe. Finally we discovered that modifying the energy flow helped. In addition, we discovered that constantly re-modulating that energy flow would compensate for the time displacement. The final step was finding a sub-frequency that would boost our energy flow and we finally found one."

Stage XII

The Arrival

Despite the complexity of all that I guess the main thing was that they could stay and help us. Phenom told me that he would have to return to the fourth dimension to oversee things there in case Denon's warriors paid them a visit. He also said that he would have Turion remain here to lead the squadrons assisting us. At that moment Turion returned with weapons for us along with eight warriors. He told Phenom that he had begun the process and the squadrons were beginning to transport to Earth. Phenom acknowledged then turned to me saying that he had to return. I told him I understood and thanked him for all he had done. Phenom stepped into the transporter and I began the cycle. Moments later Phenom vanished back to his world. All was silent for a moment when suddenly, there was a loud knock at the door.

Turion and the warriors turned and pointed their weapons at the door while the rest of us jumped up and panicked. I quickly grabbed an energy rifle from Turion and cautiously walked toward the front door. The others followed me as I got to the front door. I looked through the peep hole but couldn't see anything. I kept the chain on the door and cracked it open. It was Tom; he just got home and got my note. We all took a deep breath and calmed down. I quickly opened the door to let him in then quickly sealed the door closed again. I had him follow me to my room as I quickly explained what was going on. He quickly acquired an energy rifle from Turion. Now that we had weapons we weren't confined to my apartment. Still in doubt I asked Turion for his input as to whether we should stay in here or head outside to confront them.

Turion felt that we should go outside and position ourselves to confront them. He also pointed out that we would run out of room in my apartment. I agreed with him in that we were vulnerable staying up here and also we would run out of space in here. Steve had glanced out of the window and interrupted us. He thought he had seen them just start to reach the end of the street, the wait was over. He headed for the front door and raced down the steps. Turion and I quickly coordinated where we should position ourselves. We had left instructions in my room for the incoming warriors as they continued to transport here. When we got outside Turion and I quickly looked around to determine the best position for our troops. On the east side of my building there was a narrow path between the building and a chain link fence with some trees, bushes, and brush for cover.

Turion directed those warriors that arrived with him over to that area. He would have to stay close to the building entrance in order to direct the arriving warriors coming down the stairs. There was a small slab of concrete like a porch that went along the door entrance. There were bushes in front and along the side of the concrete slab along with a sidewalk directly in front of the door after the single step off of the porch. Turion took position there and crouched down for cover. To clarify the wishing well, it was an actual circular shaped well made of brick, but at the top it was it was covered in dirt and used for planting flowers. Along two sides of the well were four small wooden support beams. They were used to hold up a wooden triangular top made to look like a roof peak. Overall it was all made to look like a wishing well which it why we referred to it as such.

If not mentioned before, this well was in the center of a large grassy circle making the road a circle drive. However, as mentioned earlier the well was between my building and the office building directly across the street. I took position there right behind the wishing well, right in the middle of the battlefield. This would allow me access to my apartment building entrance if needed and I could better direct the Blitz team to their positions. On the west side of my building was the parking area for my building. I had Josh take position around the side of the building so he could peek around the corner toward the front of the building and down the street. I directed Christina across the street to the apartment building where the offices were. She was along the west wall directly across from Josh. There were two bushes at the corner of the east wall and the front of the office building. I directed Tom to that location where he could use the bushes for cover.

There was an open grassy area that connected to a field between the office building and an apartment building from the other complex. There were four trees in the grassy area. There was also a chain link fence between the grassy area and the building of the other complex with a narrow path. It was similar to the narrow path of my building between the fence and the building. I had Steve and Kevin take position there. As groups of warriors came down the stairs and stepped outside Turion was there to direct them into position. The entire street and both apartment complexes were beginning to take form of a battlefield. How ironic that this was happening just minutes from where my previous encounter with warriors on Earth was.

Denon and his squadron had just turned the corner at the end of the street and were beginning to make their way toward us. In just minutes the next war would begin and Earth's future would be at stake. Turion and I communicated with our hands in order to remain silent just as I did with my team. Denon and his troops were almost half way down the street and took up the entire width of the street and then some. I took a moment to quickly glance up toward my old house and noticed the foggy tunnel was still there. I didn't know if warriors from the sixth dimension were still transporting here or not. I also didn't know if any of them still occupied my old house or not but I guess none of that mattered at the moment. I don't know why but for some reason I just had a thought. *What if I could transport from my apartment to my old house*? It was a strange thought and I didn't even know if it could be done. I'd have to somehow find the right frequency in order to even try.

I needed to worry about the situation at hand. I guess I had thought about it because the idea of transporting there to shutdown that transporter had occurred to me. If I had only thought of it sooner we could have tried to transport there and could have taken Denon by surprise and possibly avoid what was about to happen. Denon and his warriors were almost to us. I refocused my attention on them and waited for them to reach us. They were at the side street just before the circle where I was. That meant that Steve and Kevin were the closest to them and they would have to act momentarily.

Christina then sneezed and broke the silence which alerted Denon and his warriors. I shook my head in disbelief and looked in her direction. She just shrugged her shoulders as if to say, "Oops, sorry dad." I looked over at Turion and we nodded our heads giving each other the signal, then we shouted out giving the order to fire. Denon and his troops were about where Steve and Kevin were positioned as Denon ordered to return fire. Steve and Kevin had to adjust their position to a more defensive posture. Denon was very well protected with a circle of warriors around him. Almost instantly there were energy blasts flying everywhere lighting up the entire area. Denon's warriors started falling quickly as we had the advantage of cover. The sky began to darken as the lightshow continued. We had to dig in and hold our positions. Pieces of brick to the wishing well occasionally went flying into the air as its structure began to deteriorate.

Denon and his warriors pushed forward causing us to reposition ourselves. There were practically right on top of us and we were quickly losing our initial momentum. I was going to have to move soon. I was a sitting duck now and at this rate there would soon be nothing left of the wishing well. The main problem was we really had nowhere to run. I looked around quickly trying to figure out where I should go. I made the decision to break towards Turion exposing me to the line of fire. I managed to reach Turion without getting hit. It was so noisy with all the firepower I had to yell in order for Turion to hear me. I hollered to Turion that we should divert some of our incoming warriors down the back stairway to the back of the building in order to reinforce the area by the chain link fence.

He agreed and sent a warrior back upstairs to my apartment to inform the incoming warriors. Denon had diverted some of his warriors toward the office building. That diversion put those warriors directly in line for Steve, Kevin, Tom, and Christina. I tried to holler to them to get out of there but they couldn't hear me. I tried to motion to them to get their attention but they didn't notice me. Steve and Kevin were retreating to the back of the apartment building in the other complex. Tom made a break for the back of the office building leaving him exposed. For the moment Christina held her position, but she would eventually have to reposition herself. Josh and I maintained our positions as the side by the street was not as exposed. By this time Trevor came out of the front door after his extended bathroom break and had no idea what the hell was going on.

As soon as Trevor stepped onto the front porch he was nearly hit. "Holy shit," he shouted as he dove to the ground. Moments later he got up and crouched down near me and Turion and joined in the fight. Denon and his warriors were getting so close and we were going to have to move, but at the same time I couldn't allow them access to the front door. It was just about dark out now which made it nearly impossible to see my team. Here on Earth we didn't glow, we were just ordinary humans, so the lack of light restricted my view of the Blitz team. We had never planned for this situation, hell I never planned for it twenty years ago. Despite the continuous arrival of energy warriors from the fourth dimension we were still heavily outnumbered.

The sky was beginning to cloud up and it almost seemed like it was going to rain. Off in the distance there were occasional faint flashes of lightning, but no rain. It was almost as if the Earth herself were feeling the effects of the invasion. I noticed that Denon had stayed back to protect himself as he sent waves of warriors ahead to advance on us. I didn't see how we were going to get out of this one alive. I glanced down at the wishing well and was glad I had moved for there wasn't much left of it. If I had stayed there I would no longer be here. All of a sudden we heard Denon yelling and his warriors shifted back toward him. I didn't understand why at first then I figured it out. Steve and Kevin had apparently moved along the back of the other apartment buildings came out from behind Denon catching him off guard. *Excellent! Brilliant move!* That was a great move and just one reason why Steve was the co-leader.

It was unfortunate that Trevor did not have his powers of illusion here on Earth. It had proved very effective in the time-zone in the past. A few moments later a warrior came running out the front door. He had been sent by Phenom to inform Turion that in fact Denon had sent an invasion force to the fourth dimension and they were in a full scale battle. I made the decision at that point to call Gannon and request assistance. Turion told the messenger to have Phenom keep sending reinforcements. With that said the messenger went back upstairs to return to the fourth dimension. I looked down the street and saw that there were no more of Denon's warriors coming down the street. That gave me a small sense of hope that maybe if we held on long enough we could hold them off, it was hard to say.

I was unable to make contact with Gannon and turned back to Turion to coordinate our strategy. Turion had moved a group of twenty warriors in front of my apartment to form a wall of protection cutting off access to my apartment. Most of my team was on the run scattering throughout the neighborhood. Things were falling apart quickly and once again the situation looked grim. Fighting on Earth just wasn't in our cards. I attempted to contact Gannon again but I could not reach him, perhaps by his design. The lightning began intensifying but still no rain as if the Earth was becoming angrier. I refused to leave the porch area. It was up to me to defend my apartment. As Denon's warriors came closer I took partial shielding from Turion's warriors to help me stand my ground. I made a third attempt to reach Gannon but again no luck. I said screw it and made no further attempts.

Denon and his warriors began to weaken and Denon began calling them off. I couldn't figure it out until I noticed that Turion and his warriors began to weaken also. We had been in battle a few hours and it occurred to me that they all needed to re-energize. Denon and his warriors were probably headed back to my old house so they could get back to the sixth dimension to re-energize. That meant Turion and his warriors would have to get back to the fourth dimension to do the same. This would present a much needed rest for us. As Denon's warriors retreated up the street Turion's warriors made their way to the front of my apartment building. He was about to tell me that they needed to re-energize when I said it for him. All of us went back upstairs and they began transporting. When it was Turion's turn to go he promised to return soon. He then transported and all was quiet.

Stage XIII

The Recon Mission

It was late and we were all very tired. We briefly sat down in the living room to talk about what just took place and what was to come. Most of the Blitz team was ready for bed so the discussion was kept short. They were overwhelmed at the intensity of the battle and I reminded them that Trevor and I tried to warn them. Tom made his way to the front door to go home when I stopped him. I said to him that I realized that he lived right across the hall but I didn't want any separation what so ever, not now because it was too risky. Tom gave a long hesitation then reluctantly agreed to stay. Tom was also a night owl so he agreed to take the night watch in Trevor's place.

As everyone else was settling in for bed I pulled Trevor aside and asked if he would join me in a little recon mission. He eagerly accepted and I spelled out my plan.

I was very determined to try and find the frequency for the old transporter at my old house. We couldn't do that at this very moment so I had thought of an alternative. I wanted him and me to drive back to my old neighborhood and attempt to get back into my old house. I wanted to see if any of Denon's warriors were left behind occupying the house. If not, then I wanted to try and find a way to neutralize, or deactivate the old transporter to shut them out. This was proving to be far worse than our last earth encounter with any warriors' years ago.

I put Tom on stand-by and we quietly exited my apartment. Once we got to my car and got in we made our way to the old neighborhood. A short time later when we arrived we parked at the end of my old street. We stayed in the car a few minutes trying to scope out the place. We couldn't see too much since it was dark out and the street was poorly lit. As far as we could tell there weren't any warriors pacing up and down the driveway so we got out and carefully made our way towards the house. We approached from the opposite side of the street as I had done the previous time. As we got closer to the house it was all dark inside. There were no lights on in the house and no signs of movement. When we got directly across the street from the house we stopped for a moment staying crouched down to study it more closely. There was still no movement from inside the house so we quietly made our way across the street onto the driveway.

We got onto the driveway and instead of going up to the front door we made our way along the left side of the house. That route took us up to the privacy gate that led to the backyard. For some reason the lock to the fence had been removed so we had access to the backyard. We quietly opened the gate just enough to slip through and walked cautiously along the back wall of the house toward the sliding glass door. We very slowly crept up to the sliding glass door to have a peak inside but when we reached the door the vertical blinds were closed and we couldn't see anything. There was a small window further down the back of the house that was to my old bedroom. I motioned for us to move that way to try and have a look in the window. We made our way past the sliding glass door and approached the small window.

We got to the window and boosted ourselves up to have a look inside. Nothing blocked our vision as we looked through the window. Although it was dark we could see the layout of the bedroom and saw no movement. It appeared is if no one had stayed behind but then we again we couldn't see everything inside. The bathroom in my old room was dark with no apparent activity from the transporter. We spent a minute looking through the window before heading back toward the sliding glass door. When we got back to it I decided to outright check the door to see if it was unlocked. No such luck, the door was locked so we moved on. There was a service door between the sliding glass door and the privacy gate. The service door led to the garage so that was the next one I would try. We reached the service door and I turned the knob and it too was locked. There was only one door left, the front door so we headed in that direction.

A few minutes later we reached the front door and I slowly turned the knob. The door was unlocked and at last we had access. We very quietly entered the front door and made our way inside. I should mention that when we first approached the house the foggy tunnel was not present. Once we were inside we looked around. It was dark and quiet with no sign of anyone here. I whispered to Trevor to split up. I would go through the foyer into the kitchen and dining room area. He would go right taking him through the living room to the hallway where all the bedrooms were. We each drew our energy rifles and began searching the house. Two steps into the foyer on the right side was a door that led to the basement. Both of us could check that later once we finished upstairs.

I passed through the foyer and into the kitchen area and things remained unchanged. Looking into the dining area I saw nothing and continued toward my old room. I reached the archway where the kitchen met the other entrance to the hallway and peeked around the corner. I saw Trevor coming up the hallway and he reported the rooms were clear. Together we carefully entered my old room and made our way toward that bathroom. We reached the doorway and I stopped in order to peak around the corner. The bathroom was pitch black. The transporter was not active so all we saw was a stand-up shower. Trevor followed me into the bathroom and for added security we shut the door and locked it before I turned the light on. After I turned on the light I stood there looking around trying to remember where the control panel was since it was not visible, it was hidden.

On the right side was the sink. Above the sink was a medicine cabinet then past that was a small space of just the wall. After that there were three shelves mounted on the wall. Below the shelves was the toilet and directly across from the toilet was the frosted bathroom window. Just past the toilet was the transporter, or should I say stand-up shower. I felt along the wall, then the medicine cabinet, then the mounted shelves looking for the control panel. *Where was that damn thing anyway?* Trevor started feeling along the other wall since he couldn't remember where the control panel was either. Finally I found it! I had forgotten that the mounted shelves were like a revolving door. I had done that to conceal the control panel when I was a kid so my parents wouldn't find it. I flipped the shelves around and revealed the control panel.

The panel was nearly identical to the panel in my apartment only more simplified. I studied the panel just for a moment to refresh my memory then I activated the transporter. I had Trevor assist me in isolating the frequency to my apartment. That process did not take long so we moved to our next step which was determining what frequency this transporter operated on. In addition, we would have to determine the transporter's wave length in order to correctly modulate the energy settings. Trevor asked if I could remember at all what frequency I had used. I could only reply that it had been too long as too many years had passed and, therefore, I could not remember. We had become focused on the task at hand and had tuned out everything around us. After working on it for over an hour I had finally found the correct frequency for this transporter and we were isolating the wave length. About thirty minutes later we found the wave length and grinned at each other in our accomplishment.

Trevor asked me since we had the frequency and the wave length what do we do next? I told him this gave us control of this transporter which we could use to prevent Denon and his warriors from returning to Earth. I also told him that once this was done we would need to take this transporter off-line and disable it in order to prevent anyone from using it in the future. Trevor mentioned that if we maintained control of it what if we used it as a backup in case something happened to the transporter at my apartment.

"So you mean if we're in the time-zone and we go to return to Earth and for some reason the transporter at my apartment prevents us from returning then we reset the coordinates and return through this one? The thought of a backup transporter to get home would be an advantage, but honestly I wouldn't want to rematerialize here to find some old lady or some dude taking a shower," I said. "I see your point," Trevor said.

Bam! Bam! Bam! All of a sudden there was a pounding on the bathroom door scaring the hell out of us. "Who is in there," a voice hollered from the other side of the door. "Holy shit," Trevor whispered. "Oh shit," I whispered back. "Open this door," the voice yelled. Trevor and I looked at each other in terror. "Who is it," I asked in a high pitched voice. "Open this door at once," the voice barked. "Shit we need to get the hell out of here," I whispered to Trevor. "How, we're trapped," he said. "There's only one way I can think of," I whispered. "Damn it we should have checked the basement and garage," I added. As the banging continued I began energizing the transporter and set the coordinates for my apartment. Whoever was on the other side of the door began trying to break the door down. When it was ready we hoped in the transporter and escaped.

Moments later we arrived at my apartment. Our arrival woke up Steve and Kevin who were sleeping in my room. I apologized for the disturbance telling them it was unavoidable. They followed Trevor and me as they stumbled out to the living room. We all took a seat as Trevor and I explained to Tom, Steve, and Kevin what had just happened not even realizing it was 3 a.m. After we explained everything to them I asked Steve if he could drive Trevor and I back to get my car. He put his shoes on and we took off. A short time later the three of us returned together and went to bed leaving Tom to finish the night watch by himself.

Stage XIV ✦ ✦

The Morning Meeting

Morning came quickly as I woke up at 7 a.m. feeling exhausted from last nights festivities. The others stayed in their slumber as I made my way around to the living room to relieve Tom. Once he wandered off to go to bed I went out to the kitchen to grab some much needed coffee. It was a couple of hours later before anyone else started waking up. As the others began waking up one by one another pot of coffee was in order. After everyone was awake and grabbed their preference of a morning beverage we gathered in the living room for a morning meeting, so to speak. At that time Trevor and I were able to fill in to the others our experience last night. At one point in the discussion Steve brought up an interesting point, something that had not crossed my mind. Steve mentioned that when we gained control of the transporter at my old house, then used it to escape, the coordinates to my apartment had been left in the control panel. This meant that Denon would have direct access to my apartment transporter.

Steve had certainly brought up an excellent point. This meant that Denon could start transporting directly from my old house to my apartment or even directly from the sixth dimension to my apartment, or both. We had a brand new potential problem and it was a big one. Based on this information I felt that we only had two options. One option was to split up the team and have half of us watch and defend the front door of the apartment building while the other half of the team stayed behind in my apartment guarding the transporter incase of a "back door" attack. The other option was to shutdown, deactivate, and lock out the transporter all together preventing Denon and his warriors from transporting here. That option, however, would prevent us from transporting also. In addition it would prevent Turion and his warriors from transporting here in order to assist us.

Neither of these options was good the more I thought about it so I presented these options to the others and asked for their input. I went around the room one by one and the others were lost not being able to decide which option was better. For the moment we were at rest not engaged in conflict. Denon and his warriors had not returned to the area so I decided that, for the moment, we would camp out here as we did before and stand watch out of the east window. After a brief period of small talk Steve suggested we begin staking out my old house like we did before. I had to think about it for a little while. I allowed it under the conditions that no more than three team members would go at a time allowing the majority of the team to remain back here at my apartment. Steve agreed saying that was acceptable and requested Trevor and Josh to go with him. I agreed on Trevor but requested that Tom go instead to give him some experience out there.

I hated to disturb Tom's sleep but I went in my room and woke him up. After the initial reluctance Tom agreed to go and got ready along with Steve and Trevor. It was almost 12:30 p.m. by the time they left. I made a quick lunch for us then afterwards I went to my room to start watching out of the east window. The kids start gamming to occupy themselves and Kevin joined me in my room so we could converse to help pass the time. A short time later the transporter became active causing Kevin and I to take action. We dove behind my bed while the kids went on alert and covered the hallway. Who would it be? Was it Turion and his warriors returning to assist us, or was it Denon and his warriors returning to attack us?

Stage XV

On the Move

The transporter finished cycling, the glow faded, and the door opened. It was Turion, along with two energy warriors. I was very glad to see him and after we greeted each other I began updating him on what had been going on. After I finished explaining everything to him Turion shared his concern and confirmed my fears. Turion said that indeed it would be possible for Denon to transport to here from my old house as well as from the sixth dimension if he had taken those coordinates with him. I asked Turion if he had any suggestions and after a moment or two he gave me an answer. He suggested that we take a small team back over to my old house and attempt to get that transporter offline. I proposed that I lead a team back over there and he, with a group of warriors, remain here at my apartment to guard this transporter and the street.

Turion pondered the idea a few minutes before giving me his answer, he agreed.

Moments later the phone rang. It was Steve calling to inform me that the foggy tunnel over my old house was beginning to return. "Shit," I hollered. "If you act quickly you may be able to transport to the house and shutdown the transporter before they arrive," Turion suggested. I asked Steve if he could see any activity at the house and his response was that he couldn't tell. I told him to reposition everyone closer to the house while Chrissy and I were going to transport over there and attempt to shutdown that transporter before Denon arrived. Steve acknowledged and kept communications open. I began activating the transporter here and had Kevin and Josh stay behind. Steve reported back saying that he had moved his minivan to the edge of the parking lot by the field.

The transporter was ready so I ended communications with Steve. Chrissy and I then stepped in the transporter. Turion would coordinate with Kevin in my absence and I energized the transporter. Moments later we arrived at my old house and began working quickly. I didn't know if there were warriors already here or not and I didn't even bother having us check. The first thing I did was have Chrissy shut the bathroom door and lock it. The next thing I did was flip around the shelves to reveal the control panel. While I was busy with the control panel Chrissy kept her eyes on the transporter while tuning her ear to any sounds beyond the bathroom door. Having already gained control of the panel on my previous visit with Trevor I immediately began working on shutting down and locking out the transporter. This had been tried more than once in the past without success. This time I had to prevail.

Suddenly my phone rang scaring the hell out of us. I was so focused on my task that I jumped, lost my balance, and fell into the toilet. Chrissy jumped up and screamed so loud it sounded like a siren going off. I quickly dried my hands off from the toilet water and stood back up to answer my phone. It was Steve calling in to inform me that he sent Trevor and Tom in for a closer look at the house. I acknowledged and quickly hung up and turned my phone to vibrate before continuing my task. Chrissy had settled down and all was quiet once again. About ten minutes had passed and I was still trying to lockout the transporter when suddenly the transporter became active. Chrissy and I looked at each other and froze.

I thought I had shutdown the transporter; however, since I had not locked it out the transporter became active; some was coming. This time it would be the opposite as escape would be through the house. I had Chrissy quickly swing the door open and after flipping the panel back around to reveal the shelves we dashed into my old bedroom. It was dark and we couldn't see since I had turned off the bathroom light on my way out. We both stumbled and ran into each other knocking us both to the ground. We picked each other up and made our way to the bedroom door. The house was quiet and seemed empty as we passed through the hallway while making our way into the kitchen. I had Chrissy contact Trevor to see just where they were outside of the house. While she did this I glanced into the dining room before peeking around the corner to look out into the foyer.

The coast remained clear when my phone started vibrating, it was Kevin. I picked up and Kevin told me that the transporter at my apartment had just been activated. Turion told him that none of his troops were set to arrive so it would not be anyone from the fourth dimension. I began to panic and told Kevin to have Turion shutdown that transporter immediately and try to lock it out since he did not have the knowledge to do it himself. In addition I told Kevin what was going on here at the house. I also told him to have Josh run outside to get a visual on my apartment building to see if there was a foggy tunnel over the building. I stayed on the line while Kevin had Josh run outside to check the sky. A few minutes later Josh returned and confirmed that indeed there was a foggy tunnel forming over my building.

At that moment Steve beeped in on the other line and when I clicked over he reported the same things Kevin just told me. I quickly told Steve to drive across the field and park at the edge of the dead end portion of the street where the four of us would rendezvous with him as soon as possible. I whispered to Chrissy to tell Trevor we would rendezvous with them at the front door. I ended contact with Steve and clicked back over to Kevin and told him that we would all be back shortly then I hung up. Chrissy and I made our way through the foyer to the front door. As we reached the front door I could hear the transporter cycle end, then we began hearing voices, Denon had returned. I had Chrissy watch our back as I quietly opened the front door. Trevor and Tom were outside waiting for us on the front porch and I could see Steve's van out of the corner of my eye parking at the edge of the street.

I tried to quietly open the door but as it opened it began creaking. The creaking was loud enough for Denon to hear it in the bedroom and he hollered, "Who is there! Go and search the area, now!" "Damn it," I whispered. I then flung the door open and hollered for everyone to run to the van as Chrissy and I ran out of the house. As we jumped off of the porch and started running toward the van I began shouting for Steve to be ready to go. Just after we got past the driveway I looked behind us and saw two warriors step onto the front porch shouting at us to stop, then they began firing at us. Moments later two more warriors joined them, then after standing there for a second they began chasing after us.

Remember my old house was the second to the last house on the street on the right so it was only thirty to forty feet to the end of the street and the edge of the field. As we approached the van Steve activated the automatic sliding side door so it would be open by the time we got there allowing us to dive inside. I looked behind us again and saw the one of the warriors that had stayed behind on the porch also began chasing after us while the other one headed back into the house, probably to inform Denon about us. Once we reached the van and dove in Steve slammed on the gas and started peeling out through the grass back toward the church parking lot. The warriors chasing us stopped their pursuit and concentrated on firing at the van. As we pulled away from the warriors I pushed the button to close the sliding door then rolled over lying down on the floor.

When we reached the church parking lot I sat up and called Kevin for an update on the apartment situation.

Kevin reported that Turion was battling the transporter cycle. Kevin said that Turion could get the cycle to shut down for a few seconds then it would start up again. At best he was delaying whoever was transporting here. I told Kevin about what had just happened at my old house and said that we wild be there in a few minutes. Kevin acknowledged and I ended contact, then I asked Steve to hurry. A few minutes later we turned down my street and as we approached my apartment building I could see the foggy tunnel fading in and out. Steve quickly got us down the street and parked the van.

Stage XVI

Our Last Stand

We jumped out of the van, darted to the front door, raced up the stair, and pounded on my apartment door. Seconds later Josh opened the door and we dove into the foyer with half of us rolling into the kitchen and the other half rolling into the living room. After a moment we got up and I ran to my room where Kevin and Turion were. I greeted Kevin and began talking to him while I started staring out of the east window as Turion kept fighting the transporter cycle. I let Turion continue the difficult task with the transporter since he was more than likely better suited for it than I was. Moments later Steve joined us while Trevor and Tom remained in the living room as Chrissy and Josh made their way to her room. I assumed Denon would be coming down the street soon with a legion of warriors so I made that point to Steve and Kevin as I refused to take my eyes off of the east window.

After a short period of time Kevin exited my room and took position in the foyer by my front door. Steve remained in my room and we continued planning some kind of strategy. Turion continued to fight with the transporter as Steve and I talked while looking out of the east window. The wind had recently picked up and was very gusty while the sky had darkened giving the appearance of approaching rain. I don't remember what time of day it was when all of this started but it was late afternoon or early evening now with a long period that had passed by since we returned to the apartment. As I continued looking out of the east window I began seeing Denon with his warriors at the far end of the street heading this way. The time had come once again.

This encounter would be very different than the previous incursion because we did not have the support of Turion's warriors. Turion continued to fight off whomever was trying to transport here but at the same time it was preventing Turion's warriors from transporting here. We were severely outnumbered and I had no idea how we were going to defend ourselves. Moments later the control panel shorted out knocking Turion to the bedroom floor and knocking him out. This same event caused the transporter to glow on and off a few times before going off-line. Steve and I rushed to Turion's side although there was nothing we could do for him. We rolled him on his back and dragged him away from the control panel. Trevor came running into my room hollering, "What the hell happened? "The control panel shorted out and knocked out Turion," I answered. "Holy shit! I heard it all the way out in the living room!"

Moments later Kevin, Tom, Josh, and Chrissy crowded my bedroom doorway to see what was going on. Denon and his warriors marched closer to my building. They were about halfway down the street at this point. With the transporter off-line this eliminated the threat of a direct transport by any of his warriors allowing us to concentrate on Denon and his warriors on the street. They continued marching their way toward us and we would have to make our move quickly. As I looked down the street from my east window Denon's legion of warriors appeared endless. There must have been hundreds of them and the situation looked hopeless. Kevin threw out the suggestion of waiting up here and letting them come to us. Once they would break the front door down there would be nowhere for us to run since the transporter was off-line. That option did not seem like a wise one.

I made the decision that we would have to go downstairs and defend the area just as we had done before. We grabbed our weapons and headed downstairs to the outside just like before. Once we got outside Steve and I began directing the others where they should go and took up a defensive position. Denon and his warriors were almost to the end of the street so we had to spread out quickly. Chrissy again was positioned across the street along the right front corner of the office apartment building. Josh again took position at the left front corner of my apartment building by the parking lot. Trevor took position along the right front corner of my building by the fence. I again ran out to what was left of the wishing well and took up position there. Steve and Tom guarded the front door to my apartment building. I had Kevin join Trevor at the fence.

Denon and his warriors were just about to the end of the street where it branched off into a circle around the wishing well. We began firing our energy rifles and the conflict began. Denon's warriors began returning fire and all hell broke loose. The warriors were not nearly as powerful here on Earth so the primary weapon on both sides was the energy rifle. This resulted in a classic ground troop battle like in the old days of war. Steve hollered for me to try and contact Gannon again but I motioned my arm back as if I was saying, "Aw forget it." On top of it all the wind grew even stronger and gust even harder while it began raining. The sky had grown much darker but not as dark as a night sky.

I could hear Denon hollering at us and throwing his arms around in a furious rage. The wishing well had taken several more hits causing the little red rooftop to be blown off and go flying away breaking a few car windows in the process. My barrier of protection was quickly withering away and would soon leave me defenseless if I didn't move. The sky continued to light up like fireworks as the rain came down harder and the sky gave way to night time. The rain, wind, and darkness did not slow down Denon's troops and they continued to close in on us. Denon's warriors were not more than forty feet or so from us making the situation even harder. Their front line would soon be on top of us and there was nowhere to escape, nowhere to run. After a lengthy period we were able to neutralize them enough to stop their advancement and both sides were entrenched.

The sustained battle lasted all through the night and into the following morning. My team and I were exhausted but the fighting would not end. The morning gave way to early afternoon when Denon's warriors began to slowly advance once again. During this whole time I didn't know if Turion had regained consciousness, or if the transporter was still off-line. Occasionally I had glanced up at my apartment windows to see if there was any activity up there but I couldn't tell. Denon's warriors had spread and were coming from that field between the office building and the other apartment complex. By that time I had noticed a few flashes coming from my south bedroom window. I had a strange feeling that the transporter was either coming back online or already back online.

A few moments later I saw Turion come crashing out of my bedroom window and fall into the bushes below. *Holy shit! What the hell happened?* It was getting hard to see because there were several small to medium brushfires all around us from all the firepower and thick smoke was filling the air. After a period of time the winds shifted and the smoke began to clear as the brushfires began to burn themselves out. I noticed a few more flashes coming from my window and felt that something was definitely happening upstairs. I looked towards the fence and saw that Kevin had been separated from Trevor and was out in the open. Denon's warriors had further advanced and were beginning to overpower us; we were about out of time. A moment later I heard a scream and looked to my left. I saw Tom get hit and fall to the ground where he laid motionless. I screamed and called to him several times, but he didn't move or respond. It was no use, Tom was dead.

"Hurry Steve! We have to seal off the transporter to keep anyone else from coming!"

"Todd, there's a group coming from across the field, they're headed right for us!"

"Alright Kevin, get Trevor back here so we can reassemble the group!"

"I can't get to him Todd there's too many warriors in the way!"

"Trevor! Trevor get over here! We have to retreat! Get back to my apartment!"

"I can't Todd I need help; they're trying to surround me!"

"Dad!"

"What Chrissy!"

"I need help!"

"Dad!"

"What Josh!"

"There's more coming from the building by the pool!"

"Damn it! Steve, you and Kevin try to get Trevor! I need to get Chrissy and Josh!"

"Todd I'm free! I'm headed for the wishing well now!"

"Good Trevor, I have Chrissy and Josh, let's go! Everyone back up to my apartment!"

"Todd they're trying to block the entrance to the building!"

"Damn it Steve!" Everyone head for the back entrance, hurry!"

"Todd watch out, there's three warriors coming out from behind the dumpster!"

"I see them Steve! Everyone hurry, get to that door! Let's go, let's go!"

"Dad, I've been hit!"

"Steve get everyone upstairs, Chrissy's been hit! I'll get her then meet you upstairs!"

"Alright Todd!"

"Chrissy here I got you, let's get upstairs."

"Alright, thanks dad."

"Steve! Steve! Get that transporter off-line!"

"I'm trying Todd, the panel isn't responding!"

"Have Trevor help!"

"Hey Todd its Trevor, everything's froze up, nothing is responding for me either!"

"Todd its Steve again, there's been a surge in the transporter! Tell him Trevor!"

"Steve's right Todd, this thing's going to blow!"

"Todd its Kevin, there's no way to stop it! We need to get the hell out of here!"

"Transporter malfunction. Destruct sequence in progress. Ten...nine...eight...seven...six-"

"Steve get everyone out now! Go! Go! Go! Hurry!"

"Three...two-"

"No!"

The computer finished the countdown and there was a huge explosion. It was like a back draft and sent everyone flying in different directions. The whole apartment building shook and the place began to crumble apart. There were several more small explosions and I landed hard on the ground. Before I knew what was happening something very large came crashing down on top of me and everything went black.